THE HORRIBLE SPOOKHOUSE

THE HORRIBLE SPOOKHOUSE

by Kicki Stridh
illustrations by Eva Eriksson

Carolrhoda Books, Inc./Minneapolis

Once upon a time, deep in the forest, there was a big, dark, horrible haunted house.

All kinds of scary creatures lived there: screeching witches, howling ghosts, and trolls with long snaky tails, not to mention the sorcerers, the wild lions, and the monsters— green, slimy, terrible monsters.

No one ever came far enough into the forest to find the house. The spooks had it all to themselves. It was rather crowded, though, what with every room filled with horrible creatures.

One day a sorcerer spotted a little girl walking all by herself deep in the dark forest. The little girl had been walking all day, looking for her mother and father. She was lost, and she was sad and tired and hungry. She had no food, and now that night was falling, she needed a place to sleep.

It was late and getting very dark when
the girl saw a light shining from the
sorcerer's window. She was so happy to
see the house, she hurried up to the door
and knocked. The little girl didn't know
that this was the horrible spookhouse.

A witch opened the door, but the little girl didn't know that it was a witch, so she asked, "May I sleep here tonight? I'm so tired. I'm lost, and I can't find my way home. I've been searching for my mommy and daddy, but I can't find them, and I'm all alone."

The witch laughed wickedly. "Of course you can stay here, my little friend. Come in, come in, if you dare. Aren't you afraid, my child?"

"No, why should I be?" the little girl answered as she came inside.

The witch was surprised, but then she realized that the little girl didn't know she had just entered a haunted house.

"I am really hungry," the little girl said. "I wonder if perhaps I could have something to eat."

The witch laughed again, "Of course you can, my child...something very, very good, hee, hee, hee."

Well, the witch thought to herself, *Now the child will be frightened*, and she led her to the kitchen. In the middle of the large kitchen, three witches stood stirring a thick, bubbling, awful-smelling soup in a big, black kettle. The witches had put snakes, spiders, frogs, snails, and worms in the soup. They stirred and stirred.

One of the witches said to the girl, ''This should be a wonderful soup, don't you think? Would you like to taste it?''

But the little girl still was not afraid. She answered
simply, ''No, thank you, I don't think I'd like it. I'd
rather just have a regular sandwich if you have one.''

And so they gave her a sandwich and milk, and
she sat at the kitchen table and ate while the witches
stirred their soup and wondered why this little girl
was not frightened by them.

When the little girl had eaten all she could, she began to yawn. She said sleepily, "Thank you so very much for the food. I think I must rest now. Is there a bed here where I could sleep tonight? I'm so tired."

"Of course," said the witch. "We have a nice little room for you, don't we?" she said, looking at the other witches. They laughed because they knew which room she meant. It was the spookiest room in the whole house. Not even a witch would dare spend the whole night there.

"That's great," the little girl said. "Thank you all for taking such good care of me."

And so the witch led her down a long, dark hallway with many doors. It was chilly and damp. Suddenly, a door flew open and a horrible monster jumped out, its gaping jaws filled with terrible teeth. The monster grabbed at the girl with its long, sticky fingers.

"Aaaaarrrgh!" the monster roared.

"Hello," the girl said, as she held out her hand to politely greet the monster.

"You really should wash your hands," the girl told him. "Your fingers feel like you stuck them in a whole bowl of jelly."

The monster stared at her in silence. He was terribly disappointed that he couldn't even frighten a little girl now that he had finally gotten the chance. He sighed and shuffled back into his room.

When they got to the stairway, a lion roared as he lunged at the little girl. His red tongue glistened in his snarling mouth.

"Oh, how lucky I am!" the little girl exclaimed. "Nice kitty cat, could you lick my hands and get all this sticky stuff off them for me?"

The lion was dumbfounded. He didn't know what to do, so he did as the little girl asked and cleaned her hands very carefully with his red tongue. Then he let her dry them on his shaggy mane.

Meanwhile,
everyone who
lived in the
house had heard
that a little girl
had come to
visit, and that it
was very difficult
to frighten her.
They were all
eager to get a
look at her, and
they all planned
to scare her as
much as they
possibly could.

By the time the witch and the little girl reached the living room, it was filled with other witches, monsters, trolls, and ghosts, shrieking and gnashing their teeth. It was enough to make anyone shiver.

But the little girl wasn't afraid this time either. She simply said, "I hope that you are all going to bed soon, because I can't sleep unless it's quiet, and I could really use a good night's sleep. See you in the morning, everyone."

The spooks could not believe their ears. Was it impossible to frighten this little girl? The witch grabbed the little girl's hand and led her down the hall to the haunted room where even the witches were afraid to go.

When the witch and the little girl finally reached the room where the girl was to sleep, the door flew open, and the ghosts rushed out. The ghosts howled and whined, and the wind blew so hard it made their hair stand on end. The witch was so scared that she nearly burst into tears.

But the little girl said calmly, "It's strange to see sheets
flying around in the air. They really should be on the bed!"
    And so she took ahold of the ghosts and made the bed
with them. Then she lay down and promptly fell asleep.
She slept soundly through the night.

When morning came, she joined the spooks in the
kitchen, where she was given breakfast—three big
sandwiches, and all the milk she could drink.

Then she thanked everyone for the food and the
bed and waved happily to them as she left.

Shortly after the little girl left the house, who
should come rushing down the hill toward her, but…

…her mother and father! They had been very worried
and had searched and searched for her the entire
night. Now they were so happy to find their little girl.

"My dear child," said her mother, hugging her
tightly, "I'm so glad you're back. Did you have to
sleep in the forest the whole night?"

"No, Mommy," the little girl answered. "I slept in
a real house, and I got food there too."

"That's wonderful," said her father, and the parents
walked their little girl home, happy that they needn't
have worried about her.

But back at the spook house, the story of the little
girl who couldn't be frightened was told for a long,
long time.

This edition published 1994 by Carolrhoda Books, Inc.

Original edition published 1992 by Gidlunds Bokförlag,
Hedemora, under the title DET HEMSKA SPÖKHUSET
Copyright © 1992 by Kicki Stridh and Eva Eriksson
English language rights arranged by Kerstin Kvint Literary Agency,
Stockholm, Sweden.

LIBRARY OF CONGRESS CATALOGING-IN-PUBLICATION DATA

Stridh, Kicki.
   [Horrible spookhouse. English]
   The horrible spookhouse / by Kicki Stridh; illustrations by
Eva Eriksson.
   p. cm.
   Summary: A little girl lost in the woods wanders into a haunted
house, where she disappoints the witches, monsters, and other
inhabitants because she refuses to be frightened of them.
   ISBN 0-87614-811-9
   [1. Haunted houses—Fiction. 2. Witches—Fiction.
3. Courage—Fiction. 4. Lost children—Fiction.] I. Eriksson, Eva, ill.
II. Title.
PZ7.S91673Ho 1994
[E]—dc20
                                                 93-22076
                                                  CIP
                                                    AC

Manufactured in the United States of America
1 2 3 4 5 6 – I/JR – 99 98 97 96 95 94